The Adventures of Amilya Rose

Father-Daughter Dance

Chavonne D. Stewart

Dogwood Farms Publications

Published in the United States of America
Juvenile Fiction
Chapter Book
Social Issues/Peer Pressure
Library of Congress Control Number: 2016904524
Hardcover ISBN 978-0-9863128-6-1
Paperback ISBN 978-0-9863128-8-5
Electronic book ISBN 978-0-9863128-7-8

Contact info: PO Box 2598 Acworth, GA 30101
theadventuresofamilyarose.com

Contents

Acknowledgements

For I am confident of this very thing, that He who began a good work in you will perfect it until the day of Christ Jesus.

Philippians 1:6 NASB

First, I would like to thank God for being my source and strength. To my family and close friends, thank you for all your love, support and encouragement. Special dedication to the best dad in the world, Pastor Joe L. Stewart.

Chapter One
Back to School

Today is the first day of school after our Christmas holiday break, and I am glad. Don't get me wrong; I enjoyed the holiday. I spent time with my family and received a lot of gifts. I was able to give gifts this year as well because I saved the money I received for making good grades and doing additional chores.

Going back to school means the school year is almost over, and I am excited about planning new adventures. Hooray! In the next couple of months, I will have time for a few more adventures before summer break.

I get out of bed quickly so I can beat my little brother Caleb to the bathroom. He tends take a long time because he likes to play in the water. This morning, I only have to brush my teeth and wash my face. I already took a bath the night before.

My school is having School Spirit Week this week, and students are supposed to wear their favorite sweatshirt today. I grab my Wyndell Elementary sweatshirt and put on jeans and sneakers. Once I finish dressing myself, I make my bed. I do my best, but I always miss a spot. Well at least I tried.

I go downstairs and see Caleb already sitting at the kitchen table. Wow! It's rare for Caleb to beat me downstairs.

"Good morning, Caleb. How are you?" I ask.

"Morning, Millie! I am good. Look, I fixed my own cereal this morning," Caleb says, showing me his bowl.

Caleb constantly reminds us that he is a big boy now, but he will still cry sometimes.

"Great job," I say with a big smile.

"Thanks," Caleb replies. "What are you going to eat for breakfast?"

At that moment, our parents enter the kitchen.

"Well, I think I might have a bowl of cereal as well," I say. I do love me some Honey O'Squares cereal.

"Kiddos, I am going to cook some cheese toast and boiled eggs. Do you want some, too?" asks Mom.

I forget about the cereal. "Yes," I say.

"No way," says Caleb.

Actually, Caleb is doing well with his cereal. Normally he picks over his food. He would rather eat candy and ice cream than anything healthy.

While Mom is fixing my breakfast, I grab a juice box out the refrigerator. This morning I choose apple juice.

"Amilya, are you ready to go back to school?" Dad asks.

"Yes, sir. I miss my class and Ms. Honeycutt," I reply.

"Great!"

"Be sure you stay focused, Amilya," Mom says. "You only have a few more months, and we want you to make A's and B's."

"Okay," I reply.

Bad grades are not an option in my home, but I am not worried. I do pretty well with my school work and even my behavior. I just have a problem with following directions sometimes. And of course my adventures can get me into trouble, but they are so fun.

I finish eating and place my dishes in the dishwasher. Caleb has already finished, so he is in the family room watching cartoons. I think about joining him, but I hear Mom talking.

"Caleb and Amilya Rose, it's time to go. Grab your bags and coats," says Mom.

"Okay," we respond.

Caleb and I love racing to the car because we want to see who will win. Before Mom can tell us to stop running, I look up and notice that Caleb beat me to the car! I guess since he has grown a little taller, he can keep up with me now. But I am still his big sister.

I giggle as Mom cranks the car and opens the garage. And then we are off. Mommy takes Caleb to Cuddle Time first, then she drops me off at Wyndell.

Ms. Honeycutt's class, here I come!

Chapter Two

The Morning Announcement

I enter Ms. Honeycutt's class. "Good morning, everybody!" I notice some of the kids aren't wearing sweatshirts. They must have forgotten about School Spirit Week.

"Good Morning, Amilya Rose," says Tommie Walker.

Wow, Tommie is speaking to me! I am in shock. He usually just stares at me like something is wrong with me or something is crawling on me. Tommie has always been weird, but I don't want to be rude.

"Hi, Tommie! How was your Christmas?" I ask.

"Great. I got a lot of gifts," he said. "How about yours?"

"Wonderful! I got to spend time with my grandparents, and of course the gifts were awesome." I don't know what else to say. "Talk with you later, got to get ready for class."

"Cool."

Strange, I tell you. Very strange.

"What was that about?" asks Leah from behind me.

I turn around. "Girl, Tommie Walker spoke to me."

"Wow!"

"I know. Tommie never speaks to anyone."

"He must have had a fantastic Christmas."

I giggle. "Yep!"

As we walk to our desk, Ms. Honeycutt enters the room. "All right, kids, get to your desks and prepare for morning announcements."

"Yes, ma'am," we reply.

All of a sudden, the bell from the intercom system chimes. It is time for Principal Bowers to give the morning announcements. He clears his throat and starts to speak. "Good morning to all my faculty, staff, and students."

I think about responding as a joke, but I don't think Ms. Honeycutt would approve.

"I hope everyone is having a great first day back to school after a wonderful holiday," says Principal Bowers. "I have a few updates about our upcoming activities for January and February. First of all, students, do not forget that this week is School Spirit Week. Today you should have worn your favorite sweatshirt. Tomorrow, we are all wearing red.

"Second, in two weeks we will have a school-wide bake sale to raise funds for the PTSA. Finally, our first annual father-daughter dance will be held on February 13. Girls, be sure to get the flyer with all the details from your teachers. That's all. Enjoy the rest of your day."

After the announcements are over, all the girls in the room begin to giggle. Patty Winslow raises her hand to ask Ms. Honeycutt a question.

"Yes, Patty," says Ms. Honeycutt.

"What is a father-daughter dance?" asks Patty, and the whole class bursts out in laughter.

"Okay, class, calm down. Patty asked a good question," says Ms. Honeycutt. "Well, Patty, a father-daughter dance is fun. You dress in your Sunday best and your father brings you to the dance. Then you eat and dance until can't dance anymore."

All the girls say, "Wow!" while all the boys say, "EEEEEWW!" Boys will be boys.

"Patty, or should I say ladies, does that answer your question," asks Ms. Honeycutt.

"Yes, ma'am," the girls reply.

"Be sure to get the flyer after class so you can let your parents know."

Oh my, a father-daughter dance! Will my dad go with me? I don't know how to dance! What will I wear? Will Christie and Leah go? I don't want to go to a dance without having some friends to talk to there. I have so many questions, and I want answers.

"Class, pay attention," says Ms. Honeycutt.

"Yes, Ms. Honeycutt," everyone responds, except for me. I am in my own little world.

The announcement about the dance has gotten me thinking. Can this be a new and different adventure? Normally, I get into trouble on my adventures, but maybe it is possible for me to go on an adventure and not get in trouble.

I have so many things to figure out, and I would rather think about the dance instead of science. Science is not my best subject because I'm not really big on bugs or rocks. The boys pay attention in science class because they like to play with bugs and critters.

Today's science lesson is about classifying animals with and without backbones. It reminds me of a fish I had in first grade. I named him Oscar. When Oscar died, I gave him a funeral. I even built him a little box to be buried in. I missed Oscar for a while, but I got over him and moved on to something else.

As Ms. Honeycutt continues to teach science, I start daydreaming about the dance. I see myself as a ballerina. I am light on my feet with a pretty, fluffy dress on. In the middle of my daydream, I feel Ms. Honeycutt eyeing me and I snap out of it.

When the bell rings for P.E., Ms. Honeycutt says, "Okay, class, put up your science books. It's time for P.E."

"YAY!" we respond.

"Get into single file. Everyone knows their duties. Randy, you are last, so you can close the door and shut off the lights."

"Yes, Ms. Honeycutt," Randy responds.

Ms. Honeycutt gives each one of us the chance to be last in line. It's like a treat to be the one to turn off the lights and close the door.

As we walk down the green hall, I think about what Principal Bowers said this morning. I start to smile with excitement. I can't wait to ask my dad to go with me! I am his baby girl after all.

Chapter Three
P. E. Class

My class goes to the field and I see Mr. Scruggs standing in his blue jogging suit with a rubber ball in his hand. I had hoped we would have free time in P.E. so I could talk with Leah and Christie, but it looks like we are playing kickball against Ms. Barrow's class. Oh, well! So much for being able to talk during P.E.

Now I have to get in my mode to win. I love to win, and I am not a great loser. Mr. Scruggs blows the whistle. In his deep, scratchy voice, he says, "All right, boys and girls. Count off by fours."

One by one we count off, one, two, three, four, until everyone has a number.

"Okay, great," says Mr. Scruggs. "Ones and threes are in the outfield first. Twos and fours are infield. Take your positions!"

I giggle on the inside because we look like little ants running into place. Roy Burn rolls the ball to the first kicker, Camielle Grant. Camielle is so prissy, and she never likes to get dirt on clothes. I remember back in first grade when Jackson and Christopher threw mud on her. She ran away crying.

Camielle is always turning her nose up at everyone, and she acts like a goody two-shoes. Before I have time to start daydreaming again, Camielle is out. She never made it to first base. I wonder if she is even capable of running fast enough to get around the bases to home.

Tim Louis is the next kicker. He thinks he is so good at sports and kicks high balls in kickball, but I always try to outdo him. When Roy rolls the ball, Tim steps back to get a good kick. There the ball goes, all the way to the basketball court!

Sam Greene runs fast to get the ball. We are all yelling, screaming, and cheering for Tim. He runs past each base and crosses the finish line. He is safe, and my team has one point. As the next person steps up to kick, I realize I got distracted by the game.

I remember that I wanted to talk with Leah and Christie, so I tiptoe away from the game. I shouldn't be missed since there are so many kids playing. I see Christie on the swings because her class got the free day today.

I walk over and sit on the swing next to her. "Hi, Christie."

"Hi, Amilya Rose. How is P.E.?" asks Christie.

"It's okay. I wanted to have a free day, but I do like kickball." Then before Christie could say anything else, I start asking questions about the father-daughter dance. "Did you hear the announcement about the dance?"

"Yes, I did."

"What did you think? Are you going to go?"

"Well, you know I don't have a father, but I do have four uncles."

I completely forgot that Christie's father died two years ago in a car accident! She doesn't talk about him much. I see tears in her eyes, and I know I need to say something quickly. I don't want my bestie to be sad.

"You should ask your Uncle Lee to go with you," I say. "He's always making us laugh."

"You're right, Amilya. I'll ask him."

"Are you going to ask your dad?"

"Yes, but I don't know how to dance."

"Do you think your mom will buy you a new dress?"

"You know my mom! I would get a new dress simply for giving her a reason to go shopping."

We both giggle.

"I wonder what kind of food the school will serve?" asks Christie.

"I hope it's not that nasty cafeteria food, "I say.

"You are so right, Amilya. That's why I bring my lunch every day."

"Hey, Christie, before I go back, do you think Leah will go, too?"

"I think she will. You can ask her when you go back to your class."

"Okay, talk to you later!" I say.

I scurry back to the field before Mr. Scruggs and Ms. Honeycutt start looking for me. I am glad P.E. is almost over. I only have two more classes before school lets out!

When I rejoin my team, I see the other team is in the lead by two points. We have two minutes left in class, and we need to score three times to win. Stacy Rowe is kicking next.

This time Lauren Waters rolls the ball. Stacy kicks but misses. After she misses the ball, Mr. Scruggs blows the whistle. For the first time in a long time, my team lost. But oddly enough, I am not worried. My mind is focused on the father-daughter dance. It will definitely be a new type of adventure for me. I am thrilled!

My class races over towards Ms. Honeycutt to line up single file, then we start our trot back to the school building. We stop at the fountain for water before entering the classroom.

After lunch, the last two subjects of the day are language arts and math. I usually do very well in language arts, and I always enjoy math.

"Class, quiet down. I know you are excited that the day is almost over," says Ms. Honeycutt.

"Yes, ma'am," we say.

"All right. Take out your homework about sentence structure."

I look through my binder and find the divider labeled English. I flip through my papers over and over again, but I don't see the paper I worked on last night. Oh, no! I know I had it. Did Caleb take it out of my notebook? No, he couldn't have. He watched cartoons all last night.

I start flipping slowly through all of my papers. Oops! There it is. I accidentally put it under the science tab instead of language arts. Wow, I was really tired last night.

Ms. Honeycutt goes over each sentence one by one, and I start thinking about the dance again. I want a new dress and shoes. Will my parents really buy me new clothes just for the dance?

Before I know it, the afternoon bell rings. I daydreamed right through math! I chuckle to myself and start to pack my book bag as Ms. Honeycutt is speaking.

"Class, be sure to complete your math assignment and study for your spelling test tomorrow."

"Yes, Ms. Honeycutt," we respond.

I whisper to Leah as Principal Bowers starts to give the afternoon announcements on the intercom. "Leah, are you going to the dance?"

"I think so. I have to talk to my mom first," Leah whispers back.

"Do you know how to dance?"

"A little bit. I take ballet and jazz at the community center, and my mom always dances with me when we listen to music. I think we are going to all have a good time."

"Me, too. I am just a little nervous."

Leah looks surprised. "Why? Your dad is great, Amilya. Do you think he won't go with you?"

I shook my head. "No, it's not that. I just have never danced for real. I mean, I can do the electric slide, if that counts."

"Oh. I can practice with you, if you want. Dancing is not hard."

Just as I am about to tell Leah she is right, Ms. Honeycutt walks around and gives all the girls in the class the flyer about the father-daughter dance.

Then the final bell rings. Ding, Dong, Ding! We all grab our bags. Leah is a walker, and I am parent pick-up. I go to meet my mom while Leah catches up with the other walkers.

Chapter Four

The Ride Home

"Hi, Mommy! How was your day?" I ask when I get in the car.

"My day was great, Amilya Rose," says Mom.

"Guess what, Mommy!"

"What?"

"The school is having a father-daughter dance. It sounds very exciting. Have you ever been to a father-daughter dance?"

"No, Amilya. Back in my day, we had Sadie Hawkins dances and proms."

"Who is Sadie Hawkins?" I ask.

My mom laughs, and I look at her with one eyebrow raised. What's so funny?

"Well, Amilya, I don't know who Sadie Hawkins is. That's just what they called the dance," Mom says.

"Is there a difference?" I ask.

"Yes, there is a big difference. Sadie Hawkins dances are for older kids, like middle school or high school. Girls ask boys to those dances."

"EEEEEEW boys! No way, no how."

Mom gives me a look with a smile on her face. "One day, Amilya. One day."

I am not sure what she means, but for now I think boys can be very mean sometimes. They are always pulling my ponytails, and I really don't like it at all. I remember when I punched Michael Brady in the stomach for pulling my ponytail. I thought my hair would fall out because he tugged very hard.

I do have one best friend who is a boy, and that's Jackson. Jackson is cool because he pretty much does what I say. That's fine by me.

Everyone in the car is quiet, and my thoughts go back to the dance.

"Mom, I have a flyer about the dance," I say.

"Great! Your father and I will read it together once we all get home," Mom says.

Read it together? This dance must be a serious thing if both my parents have to read the flyer. Questions are bubbling inside me, which is a little strange. I have never had so many questions before an adventure.

I begin to think really hard, especially about what I will wear to the dance. I like dresses. I wear them all the time on Sundays, and I wear sundresses in the spring and summer. This dress has to be very special, though. I want to look like a princess! But can I really be adventurous in a dress? I have never let anything stop me before.

Mom pulls up in front of Cuddle Time, and we get out of the car and walk inside. Caleb greets us at the door. He is always ready to go.

Ms. Ruffles is standing at the door as well. "Hi, Mrs. Patterson."

"Hello," Mom says.

"Amilya Rose, have you been on any adventures lately? Or have you been on your best behavior?" asks Ms. Ruffles

I give her a little smile and stop myself from rolling my eyes. "I've been good."

We walk back to the car with Caleb and get in. Caleb goes right to sleep by the time the car moves. I look out the window and think about the dance. I don't even know how to dance, but maybe Leah can show me.

We arrive home and Mom pulls into the garage. "Kiddos, go inside and change into your play clothes."

"Yes, ma'am," Caleb and I respond.

"We are going to have pizza, wings, and salad tonight."

Caleb and I cheer "Hooray!" and start to run into the house. In the background I hear Mom tell us to stop running, so we slow to a fast walk. By the time we finish changing clothes, I hear my father's voice. Daddy's home! What am I going to do now?

My fast walk turns into a stroll as reality hits me. I am not sure about this dance. I have never danced before, and I don't want to look crazy. I have watched music videos, but is that the type of dancing we will do?

Though I have so many questions, there is no doubt in my mind that my adventure will be a three-part sensation: I have to learn how to dance, I have pick out a fabulous dress, and I have to actually survive the dance.

I walk into the family room and see Daddy sitting in his favorite chair. I hug him and sit on his lap.

"Amilya Rose, do you have the flyer?" Mom asks.

"Oops! I have to get it out of my book bag," I say.

I hop up and run upstairs to grab the flyer, but my thoughts are fixed on learning how to dance. I have to overcome my fear. How do I learn to dance?

I can hear my mom calling me, so I go to the top of the staircase.

"Amilya Rose, what kind of pizza do you want?" Mom asks from downstairs.

"I like pepperoni pizza, with lots and lots of cheese," I say.

Before Mommy can ask Caleb, he comes from behind me and says, "Mommy, I want cheese, olives and sausage!"

"EEEW, Caleb, that sounds gross," I say, then Mom and I both laugh.

Wings aren't an issue in the family. We like a variety, so my mom always orders mild, hot, barbeque, and lemon pepper. My favorite is lemon pepper. Also, Caleb avoids eating vegetables at all cost, but I enjoy veggies, so the salad will be great as long as Mom puts cucumbers on mine.

Meanwhile, I go back to my room with my mind running a mile a minute. I have never been so afraid of the unknown when I go on adventures. I mean, I scale fences, climb trees, and walk to daycares. You name it, I have probably done it.

I decide that I need to have to have a solid plan for learning how to dance. Then I won't feel so afraid. But really, I know my daddy will love me no matter what. Who knows? Maybe he can't dance either.

I can do it! I will just have to put on some music and go for it. I giggle to myself, then I hear my name.

"Amilya Rose, it's dinnertime!" Daddy calls.

"Okay! I'm coming," I respond.

I have the flyer in my hand when I go into the kitchen. My mom is talking excitedly to my dad. I sit down next to Caleb.

"Amilya, I told your dad about the dance," Mom says. You would think the dance is for my mom. She is more excited than I am.

"Do you want to go to the dance, Amilya?" my dad asks.

I pause, then I say, "I do, Daddy! I do!"

It's like all the fear suddenly went away. What did I really have to be afraid of? Nothing at all.

Then I ask my dad, "Can you go with me?"

"Yes, Amilya. I will take off work that weekend," Dad says. "It will be a very special day for both of us."

"Amilya, you and I will go shopping for a new dress and shoes," Mom says. "And your father will wear a tuxedo."

"What's a tuxedo?" I ask.

"It is a fancy suit. Fancier than what your father would wear to work or church."

"Wow," I said.

After dinner, we all went into the family room to play UNO and Monopoly. But I am still thinking about the tuxedo. I must be very special to my dad for him to wear a fancy tuxedo. I feel a huge smile on my face.

Soon it will be time to boogie down!

Chapter Five
The Dress

It's Saturday morning and the sun is shining so bright I can feel the light on my face as I lay in bed. My family likes to sleep in on Saturdays, but today is special. Mom and I are going to the mall! We will be shopping for my first father-daughter dress.

Getting the dress is important, but today I am on a greater mission: learning how to dance. I have decided to practice dancing on my own every day for at least thirty minutes. However, later today I will be hanging out with Christie and Leah. They don't know it yet, but they will help me, too.

I have seen Christie and her father do the dance where you have to hold hands, so I will ask her what to do. I also want to surprise my dad with awesome moves on the dance floor. Maybe Leah can help me with that.

I finally leap out of bed, and I pull my sheets and comforter up just enough to make it look like I made the bed. Then I run to the bathroom so I can beat Caleb. I quickly get dressed, brush my hair, and go right into the kitchen.

I want cereal and toast for breakfast this morning, so I grab two pieces of toast put them in the toaster. I hear cartoons on TV in the family room. I didn't realize Caleb was already up! He loves Superman, Batman, and anything about cars and trains. I watch the cartoons from the breakfast table.

By the time I am done eating, my parents enter the kitchen. "Good morning, Amilya and Caleb," they say.

"Good morning," we respond.

"Amilya, I am going to fix your father and Caleb some breakfast, then we are going to hit the road," says Mom.

I giggle to myself because she said, "Hit the road." You have to know my mom. She is very serious about shopping. She calls it "retail therapy." I'm not sure what therapy means, but it must be very serious. I usually don't care about shopping. Most of the time, my mom will buy us clothes and bring them home for us to try on. If the clothes don't fit, she will return them.

Mommy turns on the radio in the kitchen as she cooks breakfast, and I hear pots and pans clanking together. An old-school song plays. She knows the song, so she starts to hum and sing while she is cooking.

The food smells so good! I guess I should have waited for breakfast, but I am so anxious to start learning how to dance. I can see myself and Dad dancing. Everyone around us is cheering and clapping their hands.

"Amilya Rose, I am ready to go," says Mom. "Are you daydreaming again?"

I laugh and say, "Yes, ma'am."

"Well, my little dreamer, let's go so we can get back in time for you to go to Christie's house."

I am excited to have some mother-daughter time. Caleb will hang out with Daddy today, so I get Mommy all to myself! I skip to the car, get in, and buckle my seat belt.

Normally, I talk or sing a tune while we are driving, but this time I ask Mom to turn on the radio.

Mom looks at me with one eyebrow up and the other down. "Amilya, what would you like to listen to on the radio?"

I pause for a second because I am not sure what I want to hear. I decide I want to hear something fast first. "Can you find a song with a good beat?"

Mom finds a station on the radio, cranks the car, and pulls out the garage. We head down the road towards the interstate. My feet and head are bopping, and I hear myself singing to the tunes.

I am so into the song that I don't realize my mom is talking to me. "Amilya Rose, are you okay?"

"Yes, ma'am," I respond with a smile. "I love the beat!"

We don't live far from the mall. My mom's favorite store is Bryant's, so of course we start there. We have to ride the escalator up to the girl's department. I start tap dancing up the steps.

"Amilya Rose, calm down. I know you are excited about getting a new dress," says Mom.

My mom doesn't understand. I am happy that I am getting a new dress, but I am more excited because I realize I do have some dance moves. All I have to do is feel the music and just move! I should be able to dance just fine at the father-daughter dance.

"Amilya, you need to focus now. I want you to pick out the right dress," says Mom.

I follow my mom through the section with all the dresses. There are so many to choose from, but I am keeping an eye on what Mom is picking up. She loves dresses with a lot of ruffles, but I don't want any ruffles on my dress. I am a big girl now.

We have only been in the girl's department for five minutes and my mom has ten dresses in her hand. She moves quickly.

"Amilya, let's stand over here so you can look at what I found," says Mom.

"Yes ma'am," I respond.

The first dress she shows me is green with a lot of ruffles. I frown. "No, no, no! That one is ugly," I say.

Then she shows me the next dress. It is a nice cream color, but it looks too plain to me. "Well, Amilya, how about this one?" she asks.

"No, ma'am. I don't like it at all. There are no sparkles," I say.

Once I mentioned sparkles, my mom put back all the other dresses and kept looking. I continue walking through the dresses, still amazed that there were so many to choose from. Then all of a sudden, I look up and let out a loud scream.

Everyone turns to look, and my mom runs over to me. "Amilya, what is it? Are you okay?" She thought I was in danger, but I wasn't.

"There it is, Mommy!" I say.

"There is what?"

I point to the perfect dress. It is hanging up on the wall. The top of the dress is black velvet with short sleeves, and the bottom is red satin with sparkles. The shape looks like a princess dress, and it has a satin ribbon that ties in the back.

"I know this is the right one for me, Mom! I want this one," I say.

"It's beautiful, Amilya. Let me see if it's in your size," Mom says.

"Okay!"

Mom goes to ask about the dress. A few minutes later, she comes back with a big smile. "Amilya Rose, it is in your size! Let's go try it on."

For the first time, I am really excited about trying on clothes! We go into the dressing room. I take off my jeans and top, and my mom hands me a slip from the rack to put on under the dress. She unzips the dress, and I hold my arms up so she can slide it over my head. As she zips it up, I am thrilled! The skirt goes down to my ankles and poofs out wide.

"Amilya, I have to find you a shawl," Mom says. "Don't move!"

Mom steps out of the dressing room quickly. Within seconds, she reappears with a black furry shawl that ties around the neck. The shawl is so pretty!

I try on the shawl, and it goes with the dress perfectly. I feel like a princess! I spin around and around until I get dizzy and have to sit down. I stare at myself in the mirror.

"This is really me!" I say, and I see my mom smiling at me.

"Amilya Rose, you are adorable! My little girl is growing up," Mom says.

I am smiling from ear to ear. Then Mom starts playing with my hair. I hear her talking under her breath about how she wants my hair to look for the dance. Then she says Dad can wear a black tuxedo with a red tie.

"Mommy, what shoes will I wear?" I ask.

"You can wear your black patent leather shoes. They will look perfect," says Mom. "Okay, little lady, let's go to the jewelry store to get you a necklace and bracelet. Also, I need to find you a little black leather purse to carry."

My mom is rambling so much that I tune out the rest of what she says. But my mind is stuck on one thing: I have to carry a purse? I usually put everything I need in my book bag, but I guess this time it will be okay.

Chapter Six

Practice makes Perfect

When Mom and I are finished at the mall, Mom takes me to Christie's house. Christie and Leah are outside playing when I arrive. As I get out the car, Mom says, "I will be back to get you at eight o'clock."

"Okay," I replied. I join Christie and Leah. "Hey, buddies, how are you doing?"

"We are good," Christie says.

"Did you get your dress?" Leah asks.

"Yes, I did. I am ready for the dance, except I have to practice my dancing," I say.

"Okay, Amilya, let's get started," says Christie.

"Practice makes perfect," says Leah.

"You are so right. I need a lot of practice," I say. "Especially with the slow dance where you hold hands."

"Have you listened to any music yet?" asks Christie.

"I have listened to some fast music with a beat."

"And you know how to do the electric slide!" Leah says.

We all giggle and go inside to Christie's basement. Christie turns her television on. It is set to a pop music channel, but she changes it to a channel with slow songs.

"This is how you slow dance," says Christie.

Christie starts showing me by dancing with Leah. "Usually, the girl puts her arms around the guy's neck, then the guy puts his arm around her waist."

"Really," I say. "I don't want a boy to touch my waist!"

We giggle louder, and Leah says, "Well, my big sister dances with her boyfriend like that all the time."

I don't have older brothers or sisters, so I miss out on a lot.

"Girls, we have to focus," says Christie. "There is a different way I want to show you. My dad taught me this way because I am short. I put one arm around his left elbow, then I hold his right hand. We step left, then together, step right, then together. We keep doing that until we make a full circle."

Christie and Leah show me, then Christie steps back. "Now Amilya, you try it with Leah."

We trip and fall the first few times, and we laugh so hard that tears fall from our eyes. But Christie makes us keep trying. Since Leah and I are the same height, I put my left hand on her right shoulder, she put her right hand on my waist, and we held hands with our other hands.

We do exactly what Christie told us to do, and it finally works. I am thrilled! Now I will be able to slow dance with my dad.

We laugh, try other dances, and play until we fall asleep on the floor. When I wake up from my nap, it is almost time to go home. My mom comes to pick me up, and I tell the girls that I will see them Monday at school.

****

The weeks fly by, and I continue to practice my dance moves. Christie and Leah have been great teachers. I am so excited that I get goose bumps on my arms just thinking about the dance.

I haven't looked at my dress since my mom bought it. It has been hanging in my closet in a dress bag. From the start, Mom said, "Amilya Rose, leave the dress alone. I don't want any dirt to get on it."

To be honest, I am not sure how dirt would get on the dress if I just look or lightly touch it. But my mom knows best, and I decide to obey her this time. My dad has ordered his tuxedo, too. He said he will pick it up the morning of the dance. I can't wait!

Chapter Seven

Father-Daughter Dance

It is the day before the big day. The week has been very long. It felt like Friday could not get here fast enough, but it is finally here!

We have three tests to take in school today: math, science, and spelling. All I want to think about is twirling on the dance floor in my new dress, but I make myself focus on the tests because I want them to be over. Then I can focus on getting ready for the dance.

The day starts out slow, but before I know it, Principal Bowers is giving the afternoon announcements. He reminds all the teachers who signed up to volunteer for the father-daughter dance to arrive at five thirty p.m. tomorrow. Parents from the PTSA will be decorating the gym.

Ding, Dong, Ding goes the bell. I rush out of the room, leaving a trail of goodbyes. I jump right into Mom's car and buckle my seatbelt, giggling the whole time.

"Amilya Rose, why are you so giggly?" Mom asks.

"The father-daughter dance is tomorrow, and I get to put on my princess dress!" I said.

"I know. I am excited, too." Mom smiles. "I have scheduled appointments for you to get your nails and hair done tomorrow morning."

Oh, wow! The only time I have been to the hair salon was to watch my mom get her hair done. Now I get to have mine done!

We arrive at the daycare, and Mom hurries in to get Caleb. Then we head home.

"Hi, Millie! How was school?" asks Caleb.

"School was fine," I respond. "What did you do today in daycare?"

"First, we had to say our A-B-C's and 1-2-3's. Then we practiced spelling our names. After all that, we got to the fun part. We played games. And, oh yeah, we had to sit down and be quiet for an hour."

"Why?"

"Well, Aidan decided to put all his toy trucks down the toilet, and I guess the toilet didn't work after that."

"What!" Mom says.

I look at Caleb with wide eyes. "Really?" To be honest, I think Caleb sounded guilty.

"Mommy, Millie, I didn't do anything," Caleb insisted.

I guess for once Caleb really didn't do anything. My mom's reaction seems to be more like she can't believe it. However, if Caleb was guilty, Ms. Ruffles would have told Mom. She tells on everyone!

Mom changed the subject. "Kids, tonight we are having hamburgers and French fries."

"Yay!" we say.

The evening goes by smoothly. We eat, watch television, and play a few games. When I go to bed, I feel like I can't sleep. But before I know it, my alarm clock is ringing to wake me.

Morning has arrived, and today is my big day! I hop out of bed, then hurry to dress. How will my hair be done at the salon? I take a look at my dress inside the dress bag before I go downstairs for breakfast.

Everyone else is already up and downstairs. Caleb is going with Dad this morning. He needs to get a haircut and pick up his tuxedo.

"Good morning, Amilya Rose! How are you feeling?" Dad asks.

"Morning, Daddy! I am great," I say, smiling.

"Are you ready for tonight?"

"Yes, sir, I am."

"Amilya Rose, here is your breakfast. We have to get to the nail salon and the hair salon," says Mom.

After breakfast, Mom and I head to

the nail salon. The lady paints my nails red to match my dress. Then she puts some sparkly polish over the red polish.

"Mommy, I like my nails," I say.

My mom smiles. This is my first time having my nails done by person in a salon. We usually have girl time at home, and my mom will paint them.

My next stop is the hair salon. Getting my hair done is okay. Sometimes it feels like the lady is combing too hard. I didn't care for that hot comb thing, either, but Mom always says there is a price to beauty. I hope getting burned isn't one of them!

I didn't know at the time, but my mom had bought me something special to wear in my hair. After the lady pulled my hair up into a bun on top of my head, she put something shiny in front of the bun. It looked like a little crown.

"What is that, Mommy?" I say.

"It's called a tiara," says Mom. "It is a miniature crown like princesses wear."

"Wow! I really feel like a princess now."

"Sweetheart, you are definitely my princess."

After we leave the hair salon, it feels like time starts to pass quickly. Before I know it, my mom is rushing to get us something to eat. She says it's almost time for me to start getting dressed. I drift off to sleep in the car.

Once we get home, my mom tells me to go wash up. "But no shower! I want your hair to stay straight."

I tell you, this hair thing is a lot of work. Just give me my two ponytails any day. After I wash up and brush my teeth, I go back to my room. My mom is waiting to help me put on my dress.

I put on my stockings first, then the slip, then the dress. Finally, I step into my black patent leather shoes. My mom already prepared my little purse. She bought me my first shiny lip gloss and let me put some on.

"Wait here, Amilya." Mom goes to check on Dad.

I look in the mirror and get lost in a daydream until I hear Mom calling my name. "Amilya Rose, you can come downstairs now."

"Okay, Mommy, here I come!" I reply.

As I leave my room and walk to the stairs, I see my dad standing downstairs in a black suit with a red tie. My mom is taking pictures with every step I take. Oh, wow, I must really be a princess!

My dad reaches out his hand to help me off the last step. "Princess, you look gorgeous."

"Thank you, Daddy," I reply.

Then Daddy brings out his other hand from behind his back. "I have a flower for you."

This flower looks strange. I've never seen a flower on a bracelet! I stare in amazement.

"Amilya Rose, this flower is called a corsage," Mom says.

"Well, Princess, are you ready to go?" Dad asks.

"Yes, sir," I reply.

My dad opens the car door for me, then he gets in. Away we go! We listen to music, talk, and laugh during the whole trip. I really feel special tonight.

When he pulls into the school parking lot, I see so many cars. Fathers and their daughters are everywhere! Before we go into the gym, we have to check in. The lady puts wrist bands on our wrists.

The gym is decorated so pretty. Since it is close to Valentine's Day, there is a big heart balloon display on the stage. There are tables covered with red tablecloths, lit candles, and little sparkles sprinkled all over.

Over to the left, I see a big buffet of food. It smells good, so I decide to go see what we are having. I see fried chicken, spaghetti and meatballs, green salad, potato salad, pasta salad, deviled eggs, cupcakes, punch, and water. Yummy! I am so glad it is not cafeteria food.

I walk a little further, and then I see Christie and Leah. Their dresses and hairstyles are fabulous. We get together and start talking. Our fathers and Christie's Uncle Lee talk, then they ask us if we want punch. We say yes, and they bring us some in fancy little cups.

Before long, we are all dancing. I dance to songs by Bruno Mars, Tim McGraw, Michael Jackson, and more. I get to do a slow dance with my dad, just like I practiced with Christie and Leah.

Then there is a dance-off contest. I am surprised that my dad has some cool moves! We come in third place. The next giveaway is for the father-daughter team who arrived first. After that, we do the cupid shuffle and the electric slide. We even do some country line dancing.

Before I know it, the dance is over. I've had so much fun tonight! I'm tired, but it was worth it. I partied like a rock star!

Daddy and I get into the car to head home.

"Daddy, I had a great time tonight," I say.

"I did, too! I enjoy spending time with my favorite princess," Daddy says.

"I'm your only princess," I say, giggling.

"You are so right."

I fall asleep in the car, and when I wake up, Daddy is pulling into the garage. He opens the car door and carries me to my room. My mom helps me get undressed, and she puts on my pajamas.

"Good night, Amilya Rose," my parents say.

"Good night," I reply.

The End

Reflection

Well, adventurers, I hope you had just as much fun as I did on this adventure. I know you are wondering what lessons I learned. The first lesson I want to point out is overcoming my fear of dancing. I had to decide within myself that I could do it, then I practiced. Whatever you start out doing, don't give up! Keep pushing forward until you accomplish what you set out to do.

Another major lesson is to all my girls: we are princesses! We rock. A princess is special, unique, and beautiful. Don't ever let anyone tell you that you are ugly. They are lying to you!

Finally, this adventure was very special to me because I got to spend quality time with my dad. We laughed, talked, and danced. Most importantly, he treated me like a princess. He showed his lovingkindness by opening doors for me, complimenting me, and always reminding me how special I am.

Adventurers, I can only imagine what my next adventure will be! So come along with me as I take on a new journey full of excitement!

About the Author

Author Chavonne Stewart is a native of Georgia, but has also lived in North Carolina and Upstate New York. She is the writer of three blogs. Real Conversation 4 Real People (justtalk4u.com) is an exploration of culture through conversation without the restraints of political correctness. The Adventureland Blog (theadventuresofamilyarose.com) provides tips for parents to help their children through the learning process while encouraging our youth to read. The Living4Purpose Blog (living4purposeenterprises.com) educates professionals on how to deal with various topics in the workplace and provide tips for individuals who are looking to make their dreams a reality.

In addition to these blogs, Chavonne founded Living4Purpose Enterprises. As chief strategist, she works in the capacity of life coach/business consultant. Her goal is to educate and empower people of all ages and help them recognize and understand their purpose in life by embracing their dreams.

Chavonne holds an MS in management from Troy University and a BA in history from Kennesaw State University. She enjoys history, DIY shows, traveling, reading, shopping, and spending time with family and friends. Chavonne is the eldest of three.

Book Reviews

The Adventures of Amilya Rose: "The Lie"

"I love your book, it sounds so much like my life...Ready for book two."

Young Reader—3rd grader

2015

"Awesome book, Best book ever!! I love your story, it has a valuable lesson."

Young Reader—3rd grader

2015

"The book was wonderful, creative and full of life lessons. Best book ever!"

Young Reader—3rd grader

2015

Coloring Page

Other Books by Chavonne D. Stewart

The Adventures of Amilya Rose: Disappearance (August 2015)

The Adventures of Amilya Rose: The Lie
(February 2014)

Amilya Rose Patterson is a witty eight-year-old with lots of personality. With her "can do" attitude and dynamic brainpower she works hard to overcome the obstacle that would keep her from enjoying her first father daughter dance. Practice makes friends perfect. In the end, what lesson will she learn?

So, friends, come along, join Amilya Rose on her next adventure.

Made in the USA
San Bernardino, CA
08 March 2017